THE BIRD
SHADOW

THE BIRD SHADOW

An Ike and Mem Story

BY

Patrick Jennings

ILLUSTRATED BY

Anna Alter

HOLIDAY HOUSE / NEW YORK

Library of Congress Cataloging-in-Publication Data
Jennings, Patrick.
The bird shadow / by Patrick Jennings;
illustrated by Anna Alter.—1st ed.
p. cm.
Summary: In spite of being frightened,
Ike and his little sister, Mem,
go with some friends to a spooky old house
with a shed full of pigeons.
ISBN 0-8234-1670-4 (alk. paper)
[1. Pigeons—Fiction. 2. Brothers and sisters—
Fiction.] I. Alter, Anna, ill. II. Title.

PZ7.J4298715 Bi 2001
[Fic]—dc21
2001016798

For Mary,
once Mary Beth
—P. J.

One Sunday, Ike and his little sister, Mem,
were playing next door at Buzzy Starzinsky's
house. Buzzy was Ike's best friend. He had a
swing set in his backyard.

"What do you want to do today?" Buzzy
asked Ike.

"I don't know," Ike answered.

"Push me higher, Ike," Mem said.

A little later, Dave Hove and his little
brother, Hugo, came over. They lived on the
other side of the Starzinskys.

"Let's go out to the Hawkins place," Dave said. "Maybe we'll see a ghost."

The Hawkins place sat out at the edge of town. The paint on the house was peeling. The grass was not cut. No one had ever seen a person go into the house. No one had ever seen one come out. Some of Ike's friends said the place had ghosts.

"I don't want to see a ghost," Hugo said.

"Me neither," Mem said.

"How about you guys?" Dave said to Ike and Buzzy. "Or are you chicken too? Bluck, bluck, bluck!" He flapped his elbows.

Ike didn't want to go. He didn't like ghosts. But he didn't want to say so. He waited for Buzzy to answer.

Buzzy didn't want to go. He didn't like

ghosts either. But he didn't want to say so. He waited for Ike to answer.

"Well, I'm going," Dave said. He took Hugo's hand and started walking.

"I don't want to go," Hugo said.

"You have to go where I go," Dave said. "Or else you can go home."

Hugo pouted. "Okay," he said. "I'll go."

"See?" Dave said to Ike and Buzzy. "Even Hugo isn't scared."

"Yes I am," Hugo said.

Ike and Buzzy looked at each other. They didn't want to go. But they were afraid to say so. So they followed Dave.

Mem had to go where Ike went.

They walked to the end of the block. They crossed Oak Street. They walked another block. They crossed Maple Street. They walked another block. They crossed Poplar Avenue. They walked more blocks. They crossed more streets. They walked until there were no more houses. There were only trees and fields and ponds. They walked past a field of yellow wildflowers. They walked past a pine woods. They came to a sign. It faced the other way. They walked past it and looked back.

" 'City limits,' " Ike read.

They were at the edge of town.

"This way," Dave said.

They walked down a dirt road. It was soft from rain the day before. They passed an old rusted mailbox. Its door hung open. The letters on it were cracked and peeling.

"What does it say?" Mem asked Ike.

"It says 'Hawk,' " Ike answered. "The 'ins' is missing."

They came to an old wooden sign hung on an old fence. The letters on it were cracked and peeling.

Ike read it to Mem: " 'Trespassers beware!' "

"What are trespassers?" Mem asked.

"People who go where they don't belong," Ike said.

"Like when I go into your room?" Mem asked.

"You can go into my room," Ike whispered. He didn't want Dave to hear him. "Just ask first."

"I want to go home," Hugo said.

"Don't be a baby," Dave said.

Hugo scowled at him. "I'm not a baby," he said to himself.

Buzzy looked at his watch. "It's five o'clock," he said. "I have to get home. Supper's at six."

"Bluck, bluck, bluck!" Dave said. He flapped his elbows. He walked up the drive toward the Hawkins place. He pulled Hugo along with him.

Ike looked at Buzzy. Buzzy looked at Ike. Ike didn't want to follow Dave. Buzzy didn't want to follow him either. But they followed him.

The paint on the Hawkins house was peeling. Its windows were cracked. The grass was not cut. Beside the house was a small shed. "Coo, coo, coo," the shed said.

"It's ghosts!" Mem said. She stood behind Ike and sucked her finger.

They all stepped quietly around the shed. There was a window on the other side. Dave peered in. Ike and Buzzy peered in too. Mem and Hugo were too short.

"Look at that!" Dave said.

"That's weird," Buzzy said.

"What are they doing in there?" Ike said.

"Let me see!" Mem said. She tugged on Ike's shirt. "Is it ghosts?"

Ike boosted Mem up. They looked in the window. They saw lots of birds. They were all gray. They all sat very still. "Coo, coo, coo," they said.

"Pigeons," Ike said.

"How did they get in?" Mem asked.

"Let me see!" Hugo said. He tugged on Dave's shirt.

"Knock it off!" Dave said. He pushed Hugo away.

"Here, Hugo," Buzzy said. He locked his hands together. Hugo put his foot in Buzzy's hands. His shoe was muddy. Buzzy boosted him up.

"I think they're trapped," Dave said. "We should let them out."

He tried to open a window. It wouldn't open. He tried the door. It wouldn't open either. It was locked.

"I think we should go," Ike said.

"Go ahead, chicken," Dave said. "I'm going to let them out!"

He picked up a rock and threw it at the window. There was a very loud crash.

"Coo! Coo! Coo!" said the pigeons.

"Let's get out of here!" Dave yelled, and ran away from the shed. He ran away down the drive. He did not wait for Hugo.

Hugo began to cry. Buzzy took his hand.

"It's okay," Buzzy said to him. "Come on." They ran down the drive together.

Ike took Mem's hand and ran too. They all ran past the sign that said TRESPASSERS BEWARE! They ran past the old rusted mailbox that said

HAWK. They ran down the soft dirt road. They stopped at the sign that said CITY LIMITS.

"I saw somebody," Mem said, out of breath.

"What do you mean?" Dave said. "Where?"

"In the window," Mem said. "In the house."

"What house?" Dave asked.

"At the Hawkins place," Mem said.

"Maybe it was a *ghost!*" Dave said spookily. He pretended to be scared. Then he laughed. "Come on, Hugo," he said. He took Hugo's hand from Buzzy's. "We better get home for supper." He led Hugo away. Hugo looked back and waved.

"Bye, Buzzy," he said.

Buzzy waved back.

"I *did*," Mem said to Ike. "I *saw* somebody."

Ike looked into Mem's eyes. She was

telling the truth. He could tell.

"Maybe we should go back," Ike said.

"Why?" asked Buzzy.

"I don't know," Ike said.

Buzzy looked at his watch. "I have to go!" he said. "I'll be late for supper!" And he ran away down the street.

"Do you think we should go back?" Ike asked Mem.

"What if it was a ghost?" Mem asked.

"Did it look like a ghost?" Ike asked.

"It looked like a man," Mem said.

"We better go back," Ike said.

They walked back down the soft dirt road,
past the old rusted mailbox that read HAWK
and the TRESPASSERS BEWARE! sign. They
walked up the drive to the Hawkins place. Ike
peered in the shed's broken window.

"They're still there," Ike whispered. "They
didn't fly away."

"Let me see," Mem whispered.

Ike boosted her up. She saw the pigeons.
They sat very still. "Coo, coo, coo," they said.

"Why do they stay inside?" Mem asked.

"They can get out now."

"They don't want to get out," a voice from behind them said. They turned around and saw a man in brown overalls and a brown hat standing above them. He had a gray beard. He had a cane. He put his hand on Ike's shoulder.

"Which of you kids broke my window?" he asked.

Ike was too scared to answer.

"I saw you kids," the man said. "I saw you from the house. I saw you all run away."

"It wasn't *us!*" Mem said. She was very scared too.

"I'm going to have to call your folks," the man said. He bent down and looked into Ike's eyes. "What's your name, son?" he asked.

Ike couldn't remember his name.

"He is Ike," Mem said. "I'm Mem."

"And what's your phone number?" the man asked.

Ike couldn't remember his phone number.

"Six-six-three, three-four-six," Mem said.

"That's only six numbers," the man said. "Phone numbers have seven."

"That's our number," Mem said. "I know our number."

"No matter," the man said. "I can find you. I can find anyone."

"Coo, coo, coo," said the pigeons.

"You kids better be getting home," the man said. "Tell your folks I'll be calling."

"Yes, sir," Ike said.

Ike took Mem's hand and they ran away down the drive. They ran past the TRESPASSERS BEWARE! sign, and the old rusted mailbox that said HAWK, and down the soft dirt road. They ran past the sign that said CITY LIMITS. They ran past the pine woods and the field of yellow wildflowers. They ran many blocks. They crossed many streets. They walked while crossing. They crossed Poplar Avenue and Maple Street and Oak Street. Finally, they were home. The car was in the drive.

"Daddy's home!" Mem said.

Ike and Mem went around to the back door and stepped into the kitchen.

"Look at your shoes!" Ike's mother said to them. "They are covered with mud!"

Ike and Mem looked at their shoes. They were covered with mud.

"Sorry, Mom," Ike said. He led Mem outside. They took off their shoes and left them on the patio.

"Are you going to tell Mommy and Daddy?" Mem whispered to Ike.

"Shhh," Ike said. He wanted to tell his mother and father about the Hawkins place. He wanted to tell them about the pigeons and the window. But he was scared. He was scared of Dave Hove. He was scared of the man at the Hawkins place. And he was scared of getting in trouble.

"No," Ike whispered to Mem. "The man can't call us. You didn't give him the whole number. Don't say anything, Mem, okay? Don't say anything about the Hawkins place to Mom and Dad. Don't say anything to anyone, okay?"

"Okay," Mem said. "I won't."

Ike's mother made spaghetti for dinner. Spaghetti was Ike's favorite, but he couldn't eat. He just stabbed at his food with his fork, and waited for the phone to ring. He waited for a knock at the door. The man at the Hawkins place said he would find him. He said he could find anyone.

"What did you do today?" Ike's father asked.

"Nothing," Ike said.

"Nothing," Mem said too.

After dinner Ike tried to do his math

homework, but he couldn't think straight. He could only think about the man at the Hawkins place. He closed his math book and opened his library book. It was a story about an octopus that played shortstop. He tried to read it, but he couldn't think straight. He could only think about the pigeons. He could almost hear them cooing: "Coo, coo, coo." He closed his library book.

Mem knocked on his door.

"Can I come into your room, Ike?" she asked.

"Sure," Ike said.

Mem sat on the edge of his bed. "What are you doing?" she asked.

"Reading," Ike said.

"But your book is shut," Mem said.

"I'm finished," Ike said.

"What book is it?" Mem asked. "Does it have ponies?"

"No," Ike said. "It's about an octopus that plays baseball."

"Is it a boy octopus or a girl octopus?" Mem asked.

"It's a boy octopus," Ike said.

"Does he wear a cap?" Mem asked.

"Uh-huh," Ike said.

"Does he wear a mitt?" Mem asked.

"He wears seven of them," Ike said.

"Coo, coo, coo" came a voice from somewhere.

"What did you say?" Ike asked Mem.

"I didn't say it," Mem said. "Somebody else did."

"Coo, coo, coo," the voice said again.

"It's coming from the window," Ike said.

He stood up from his desk and walked to the window. A pigeon was perched on the ledge. "Coo, coo, coo," it said.

"It's a pigeon," Mem said.

"I know it's a pigeon!" Ike said. He opened the window. The night air was chilly. "Shoo! Shoo!" he said. The pigeon flew away. Ike shut the window. The pigeon came back.

"It's back," Mem said.

"I know it's back!" Ike said. He opened the window. "Shoo! Shoo!" he said. The pigeon flew away. Ike shut the window. The pigeon came back.

Mem didn't say anything.

"Ike! Mem!" Ike's mother called from the bottom of the stairs. "Bedtime! Don't forget to brush your teeth!"

"Okay, Mom!" Ike called back.

"Okay, Mommy!" Mem called too.

"You don't need to come up!" Ike called. "I'll get Mem's pajamas on her!"

"Thanks, honey!" Ike's mother called. "Come down after and say good-night!"

"Okay, Mommy!" Mem called.

Ike got Mem into her pajamas. He got into his own. They brushed their teeth. Then they went downstairs.

"Well," Ike's mother said. "All ready for bed."

"Yes, ma'am," Ike said. He kissed his mother's cheek. He hugged his father.

"Good night, Mommy," Mem said. She kissed her mother's cheek. She hugged her father.

"Good night, Mem," he said.

"Rrrrring!" the phone said.

Ike and Mem froze.

"Maybe that's *him!*" Mem gasped.

Ike's father picked up the receiver. "Hello?" he said. "Oh, hi, Phil."

Ike breathed a deep sigh. So did Mem. Phil was just Ike's father's friend. They bowled together sometimes.

"Maybe that's *who?*" Ike's mother asked Mem.

"No one," Ike said.

"No one," Mem said too.

"Come on, Mem," Ike said. "Let's go up."

They ran upstairs. Ike tucked Mem in. Then he went to bed. The streetlight shined in his window. A big bird shadow danced on his wall.

"Coo, coo, coo," the pigeon said.

Ike pulled his blanket up over his face.

The pigeon was still there in the morning. It sat on the kitchen window ledge while Ike and Mem ate their cereal.

Ike went to the window and opened it. The morning air was chilly. "Shoo! Shoo!" he said. The pigeon flew away. Ike closed the window. The pigeon came back.

It followed Ike and Mem as they walked to school. It waddled along the sidewalk behind them, bobbing its head. "Coo, coo, coo," it kept saying.

"Shoo! Shoo!" Ike kept saying. But the pigeon wouldn't shoo.

"She's funny," Mem said. "I'm going to call her Debbie."

"Like Debbie Antcliff?" Ike asked. "Your best friend at school?"

"Yes," Mem said. "Debbie Antcliff walks like that. She's funny too."

"How do you know it's a girl pigeon?" Ike asked.

"Because she walks like Debbie Antcliff!" Mem said.

Mem took her sandwich out of her lunch box. She gave some bread crumbs to Debbie. Debbie ate them up.

"Coo, coo, coo," she said.

"Coo, coo, coo," Mem said.

Debbie tried to follow Ike and Mem into the school, but Ike blocked her with his foot. Then Gina Poppick opened the door and Debbie scooted in. She followed Ike and Mem down the hall.

"Shoo! Shoo!" Ike said. But Debbie wouldn't shoo.

"Hey, Ike!" Steve Sipe said. "Your girlfriend is following you!" He laughed. Some other kids did too.

Ike dropped Mem off in the preschool. Her best friend, Debbie Antcliff, was at the door waiting for her. Then Ike walked to his room. Ike was in Mrs. Quibble's second grade class. Dave Hove was standing by the door.

"Did you tell?" Dave whispered to Ike. But before Ike could answer, Dave saw Debbie.

His eyes opened very wide. His mouth opened very wide.

Suddenly, the pigeon flew up over their heads. She flew into the classroom.

"Shoo! Shoo!" Ike said. But Debbie wouldn't shoo.

The bell rang. All the children sat down at their desks. Mrs. Quibble sat at her desk. Debbie sat on Ike's desk.

"Coo, coo, coo," she said.

"It's a pigeon!" Buzzy gasped.

"I know it's a pigeon!" Ike said.

"Oh my!" Mrs. Quibble said. "There's a bird in the school! Oh my, oh my! That's very bad luck! Shoo! Shoo!" She waved her hands. She opened the window. She stomped her feet. But the pigeon wouldn't shoo.

Mrs. Quibble went and got Mr. Bookwalter. He caught Debbie in a cardboard box.

"I'll let it loose outside," he said, smiling. He carried the box out of the classroom.

Ike sighed.

Mrs. Quibble collected the math homework.

"Where's your homework?" Mrs. Quibble asked Ike.

"I couldn't think straight last night," Ike answered.

"Well, stay in today at recess," Mrs. Quibble said. "I'll help you think."

"Yes, ma'am," Ike said.

"Coo, coo, coo" came a voice from somewhere. It was Debbie. She was in the window.

As always, Ike's mother picked Mem up at lunchtime. Ike walked home in the afternoon, but he was not alone. Debbie followed him.

Ike got his ball and mitt and went to the baseball field. Debbie followed him. She ran around the bases behind him. She stood in the outfield with him. She cooed whenever he caught a fly ball.

Ike told Buzzy about the man at the Hawkins place.

"Did you tell your mom anything?" Buzzy asked Ike.

Ike shook his head. "Did you?" he asked.

Buzzy shook his head. "She would kill me."

"Yeah," Ike said.

When Ike left the baseball field, Debbie did too. When Ike went up to his room to change, Debbie was in his bedroom window. When he went into the bathroom to wash up, Debbie was in the bathroom window. When Ike went down to supper, his mother was boiling hot dogs.

"We're eating at the counter tonight," she said. "Mem wants to play hot dog stand."

Mem was sitting on a stool. Ike's father was sitting beside her on another one. There were squeeze bottles on the counter. One was red. The other was yellow. Ike's mother set a hot dog on Ike's plate.

"Coo, coo, coo" came a voice from somewhere.

"What's that?" Ike's father asked.

Mem pointed at the kitchen window. "It's Debbie!"

Ike went to the window and opened it. Debbie flew into the kitchen. She flew over the counter. She flew over the hot dogs. She settled down on Ike's stool.

"Coo, coo, coo," she said.

"Her name is Debbie," Mem said. "Because she walks like Debbie Antcliff." Mem tore off a piece of her hot dog bun and put it on Ike's stool. Debbie pecked at it.

"I have to tell you something," Ike said to his parents.

And he told them about the Hawkins place.

He told them about the pigeons. He told them about Dave and the window. He told them about Debbie.

After dinner, Ike's father spoke to Dave's father on the phone.

"Dave is going to kill me," Ike said.

"He better not," Mem said.

"He won't," Ike's mother said with a smile.

Then the family climbed into the car. Debbie climbed in too. They drove past the fields and ponds, past the yellow wildflowers and the pine woods. They drove past the sign that said CITY LIMITS. They turned onto the soft dirt road. They drove past the old rusted mailbox that said HAWK and the sign that said

TRESPASSERS BEWARE! They drove up the drive to the Hawkins place.

"Coo, coo, coo!" Debbie said when the car stopped.

Ike opened his door and Debbie flew out. She flew to the shed. She flew in through the broken window.

The man came out of the house. He wore brown overalls and a brown hat. He walked with a cane. "Evening," he said.

"Evening," Ike's father said. He shook the man's hand. "I'm John Nunn," he said. "And this is my wife, Laurie."

"Hello," Ike's mother said.

The man tipped his hat. "Pleased to meet you," he said. "The name is Hawkins. Culver T. Hawkins."

"Well, Mr. Hawkins," Ike's father said.

"My son wanted to tell you that he's sorry about your window. Didn't you, Ike?"

"Yes, sir," Ike said. "I'm sorry, Mr. Hawkins."

"Me too," Mem said.

"I thought you said you didn't break my window," Mr. Hawkins said to them.

"We didn't!" Mem said.

"But we did run away," Ike added. "I guess we were scared."

"Of *ghosts?*" Mr. Hawkins said spookily.

"Do you really have some?" Mem asked.

Mr. Hawkins smiled. "No. But I do have birds. Would you like to meet them?"

"Sure!" Mem said.

Mr. Hawkins showed Ike and Mem the pigeon coop. He said the pigeons were his pets. He said that they fly away sometimes.

"But they always come back," he said.

Mem picked out Debbie right away. She was the one that walked like Debbie Antcliff.

Soon it began to get dark. Ike's mother said it was time to leave.

"We don't want to leave yet," Ike said.

"No," Mem said. "Debbie likes us."

"Well, you can come and visit anytime," Mr. Hawkins said. "If that's okay with your folks, that is."

"Of course," Ike's mother said.

Ike and Mem smiled.

Just then a car drove up the drive.

"It's Dave!" Ike whispered to Mem.

Mr. and Mrs. Hove got out of the front seat. They didn't look happy. Mr. Hove was holding a checkbook. Dave and Hugo got out of the backseat. They didn't look happy either. Dave glared at Ike.

"Don't kill Ike, Dave!" Mem said.

Everybody laughed—everybody but Dave and Ike.

That night Ike put on his pajamas and brushed his teeth. He turned out his light and got into bed. The streetlight shined in through his window onto the floor. There was no big bird shadow. There was no cooing. Ike felt sad.

The next day Ike and Mem walked to school alone.

"I miss Debbie," Mem said.

"Me too," Ike said.

Dave didn't say a word to Ike all day. He just glared at him. Ike pretended not to notice.

After school Ike played baseball with Buzzy. Dave and Hugo were there too. Dave didn't talk to Ike, but Hugo did.

"Dave has to pay for the window out of his allowance," he said.

"Is he going to kill me?" Ike asked.

"Maybe," Hugo said. "But I'll be on your side."

"Me too," Buzzy said.

"Thanks," Ike said.

When Ike got home, he and Mem walked to the end of their block. They crossed Oak Street. They walked another block. They crossed Maple Street. They walked another block. They crossed Poplar Avenue. They walked more blocks. They crossed more streets. They walked until there were no more houses. There were only trees and fields and ponds. They walked past a field of yellow wildflowers. They walked past a pine woods. They came to a sign. It faced the other way. They walked past it and looked back.

" 'City limits,' " Mem said.

They were at the edge of town.

They walked down a dirt road. It was hard and dry now. The day had been warm and sunny. They passed an old rusted mailbox. Its door hung open. The letters on it were cracked and peeling.

" 'Hawk,' " Mem said.

"The 'ins' is missing," Ike said.

They passed an old wooden sign hung on an old fence. The letters on it were cracked and peeling.

" 'Trespassers beware!' " Mem said.

They walked up the drive to the Hawkins place. They walked past the pigeon coop. The glass in the window had been replaced. They walked up to the house. Ike knocked on the door. A few minutes later, Mr. Hawkins opened it.

"Well, hello!" he said. "Come to see the birds?"

Ike and Mem both nodded.

Mr. Hawkins opened the coop and one of the pigeons flew out. It was Debbie. Mem fed her bread crusts from her lunch box. Then she and Ike ran around the yard in the tall grass. Debbie followed behind them. They ran up and down the drive. Debbie followed. They climbed a tree. Debbie flew up and sat on the branch beside them.

"Coo, coo, coo," Debbie said.
"Coo, coo, coo," Ike said.
"Coo, coo too!" Mem said.